"We could do it!"

saving their lives."

"We might get a big reward," Huey said.

"We'd be heroes," I said.

YOUNG CORGI BOOKS

Young Corgi books are perfect when you are looking for great books to read on your own. They are full of exciting stories and entertaining pictures. There are funny books, scary books, spine-tingling stories and mysterious ones. Whatever your interests you'll find something in Young Corgi to suit you: from families to football, from animals to ghosts. The books are written by some of the most famous and popular of today's children's authors, and by some of the best new talents, too.

Whether you read one chapter a night, or devour the whole book in one sitting, you'll love Young Corgi books. The more you read, the more you'll want to read!

Other Young Corgi books about Julian and Huey
THE JULIAN STORIES
JULIAN, DREAM DOCTOR
BANANA SPAGHETTI
HUEY'S TIGER

Julian, Secret Agent

Ann Cameron

Illustrated by Lis Toft

JULIAN, SECRET AGENT
A YOUNG CORGI BOOK 0552 548235

First published in the USA 1990 by Random House, Inc
First published in Great Britain 1992 by Victor Gollancz Ltd
Published in Corgi Yearling 1994
This edition published by Young Corgi Books,
an imprint of Random House Children's Books, 2002

3 5 7 9 10 8 6 4 2

Cover illustration by Lis Toft

Papers used by Random House Children's Books are natural, recyclable products made from wood grown in sustainable forests. The manufacturing processes conform to the environmental regulations of the country of origin.

Young Corgi Books are published by Random House Children's Books,
61-63 Uxbridge Road, London W5 5SA,
a division of The Random House Group Ltd,
in Australia by Random House Australia (Pty) Ltd,
20 Alfred Street, Milsons Point, Sydney, NSW 2061, Australia,
in New Zealand by Random House New Zealand Ltd,
18 Poland Road, Glenfield, Auckland 10, New Zealand,
and in South Africa by Random House (Pty) Ltd,
Endulini, 5A Jubilee Road, Parktown 2193, South Africa

THE RANDOM HOUSE GROUP Limited Reg. No. 954009

A CIP catalogue record for this book is available from the British Library.

Printed and bound in Great Britain by
Cox & Wyman Ltd, Reading, Berkshire.

In memory of Ernst Hacker –
and for everyone who dares
to dare

A.C.

Contents

Crimebusters

It was a morning when the sun stayed in bed.

It was a morning when the clouds had pillow fights.

It was a morning when it looked like it could rain rubber boots, submarines, lost pirate ships, sunken treasures, or a whole new world.

My best friend, Gloria, my little brother, Huey, and I were in the post office, posting some letters for my mother. When we finished, the rain started. We couldn't leave.

We were alone in the post-office lobby. The rain was pounding down on the roof.

Gloria and I stared out of a window. We couldn't see anything but water.

'This is like living in an aquarium!' Gloria said.

'When can we go home?' Huey asked.

'Don't worry!' I said. 'Someday – tomorrow, next week, next month – it's got to stop raining.'

We looked around the lobby. There was a poster explaining how to collect stamps. There was a notice about how much it cost to post things. There was a bunch of papers hanging on a hook on the wall.

Gloria took the papers off their hook. We looked at them over her shoulder.

Every page had a set of fingerprints at the bottom and two photos of a person in the middle. In big letters at the top of each page it said WANTED. CITIZEN'S ALERT.

'Reports on criminals!' I said.

'Right!' Gloria said. She started reading out loud. ' "Evelyn Gertrude Smith. Held up freeway tollbooths in Ohio. Stole seven thousand five hundred thirty-one dollars and twenty-five cents in quarters.

‘ “Ernest ‘Moonface’ Wallace. Rustles cattle to save them from slaughterhouses. Sells them to rodeos.

‘ “Eugene George Johnson, ‘the Great Imitator’. Twenty-one years old. Uses many names. Has struck in thirty-two states. Robs banks while pretending to be bank worker. Has photographic memory. Talks in a strange private language. Also speaks Chinese. Five feet ten inches tall. Has small scar above right upper lip. Hobby: cooking. Twenty-five-thousand-dollar reward for his capture.

‘ “Mildred Miller. Grade school art teacher. Hijacked airplane in Oregon. Parachuted out over Montana with all the passengers’ money and jewels.” ’

Gloria stopped reading. ‘How could a *teacher* become a criminal?’ she asked.

‘Remember Miss Reasoner?’ I asked. ‘Our art teacher? Remember the day Bobby Sloan filled a water pistol with paint? He accidentally squirted it in her hair when he was aiming for somebody else. Remember when she took his squirt gun away? She said, "You children may drive me to crime!" '

'But Miss Reasoner wouldn't ever become a criminal!' Gloria said.

'Maybe not,' I said. 'But there sure is a lot of crime around.'

'A crime could happen right here,' Gloria said.

'Look how dusty these papers are!' I said. 'Nobody has read them in weeks.'

'Grown-ups should be studying these! They should keep up on crime!' Gloria said.

'It's too bad grown-ups aren't more like us,' I said. 'We'd be great at catching criminals.'

'We would?' Huey asked.

'Of course we would!' Gloria said.

'We could do it!' I said. 'We could be secret agents. Nobody would even notice us, because we're kids. And all the time, we'd be protecting people –

maybe even saving their lives.'

'We might get a big reward,' Huey said.

'We'd be heroes,' I said.

'It's lucky we have bikes,' Gloria said. 'We can hunt for criminals all over town.'

'All over town?' I said.

'Sure!' Gloria said.

'There's just one problem,' I said. 'Dad told us he doesn't want us to go too far from home this summer.'

'How far is "too far"?' Gloria asked.

'I don't know.'

'Look at it this way,' Gloria said. 'We won't go to New York. We won't go to Paris. If we find a criminal leaving for Tokyo, we just won't follow her. So, we won't *go* far from home.'

I thought about it. I thought about accidentally going someplace Dad wouldn't like – and then saying, 'Dad, we thought *far* meant Tokyo.' I didn't know how he would take it.

'Julian,' Gloria said. 'What trouble could we get into?'

‘I don’t know,’ I said.

Actually, I couldn’t see any trouble coming. But that’s how I am about trouble.

‘All right,’ I said. ‘We’ll do it. We’ll be crimebusters.’

I went to the window. It had stopped raining. The sun had come out. It looked like a whole new world.

We Talk Things Over

We got on our bikes and rode to the city park. Huey rode on the back of my bike. We sat on the steps by the statues, where no-one could hear us, and started planning.

'We need a motto,' I said.

' "All for one, one for all," ' Gloria

said. 'We'll stick together, no matter what happens! No matter how big the danger!'

'We need a secret code,' Huey said.

'How about a warning?' I suggested. 'Always alert.'

Gloria and Huey nodded.

'If we see danger,' I said, 'we'll say, "AA". If you hear us say that, Huey, it will mean you should stop talking.'

'OK,' Huey agreed.

I was glad. If Huey stopped talking when I said 'AA' I wouldn't have to step on his foot any more to stop him. The way things were, sometimes I stepped on his foot too hard. Even worse, sometimes I couldn't reach it to step on.

'If a situation is too dangerous,' Gloria said, 'we need an escape code.'

'Make like a tree, and leave,' I suggested.

'Or just, make like a tree,' Gloria said. 'That's faster. Can you remember it, Huey?'

'Make like a tree!' Huey said, and

he wiggled his hands in the air like leaves.

'Remember, Huey, if we say, "Make like a tree!" – run!'

Huey said he would.

I figured we were ready for practically anything.

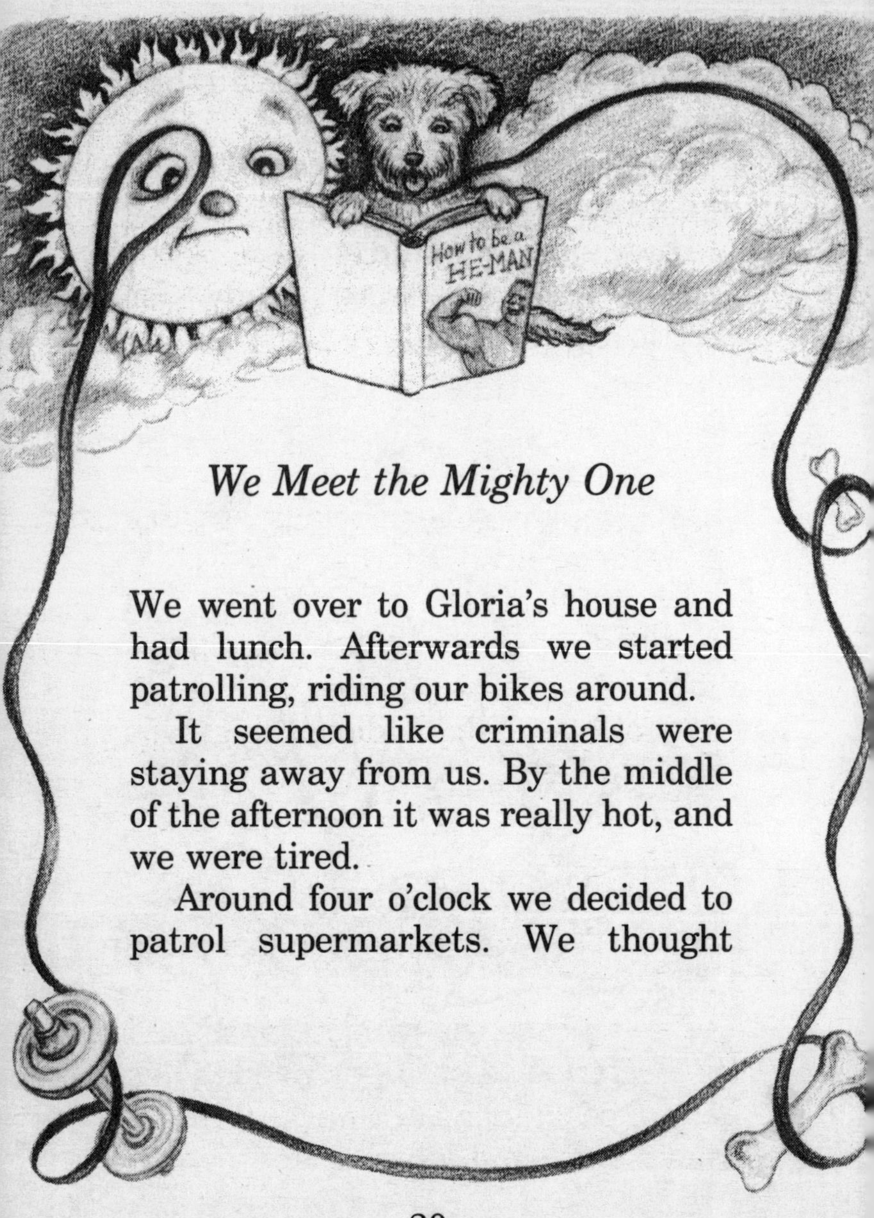

We Meet the Mighty One

We went over to Gloria's house and had lunch. Afterwards we started patrolling, riding our bikes around.

It seemed like criminals were staying away from us. By the middle of the afternoon it was really hot, and we were tired.

Around four o'clock we decided to patrol supermarkets. We thought some criminal might go there to get food and take it back to his hideout.

Everything was normal in the first three supermarkets – kids crying, mothers or dads pushing shopping trolleys, kids trying to ride the trolleys like scooters, people knocking over hundreds of cans of tuna fish, kids *demanding* a certain kind of sweet they'd seen advertised on TV.

The fourth supermarket was one I'd never been to before.

We patrolled the same way we had patrolled the others – checking the car park first, looking for guns in the back seats of cars, dead bodies, things like that. No luck.

We stopped and looked at a dog inside a car.

'Isn't he cute?' Gloria said. She wants a dog even more than Huey and I do.

She touched the window glass, and the dog tried to sniff her hand. Then he looked at her very hard with big brown eyes, and whined, and panted a little, and panted a little more. He put his paws against the window.

A woman came up behind us. 'It's a crime!' she said.

'We aren't doing anything!' Huey said.

'Not you,' the woman said. 'The car. The dog. The windows. It's a crime!'

She pushed by us and went towards the store.

'What's the crime?' Huey said.

'We have to investigate,' I said.

'Here, pooch!' Gloria called, and put her hand against the window. But the dog didn't jump up again. He just looked at Gloria, and whined, and dropped his head against the seat.

'That dog is sick,' Gloria said.

'It must be really hot in the car,' Huey said.

'I wonder how long he's been in there,' I said.

'He needs to get out,' Gloria said. 'The sun has made that car like an oven. That's what the crime is – that he can't get out. We have to tell the person who owns the car!'

'Let's get the licence number!' I said.

We went around to the front of the car to find the licence plate. Gloria wrote it down: MIGHTY-1.

Then we went into the store and asked for the manager.

A small man came down from the high booth where the money and receipts are kept.

'I'm the manager,' he said. 'What can I do for you?'

'It's about a dog,' I said. 'A dog stuck in a car. The windows are closed, and he looks sick.'

'He probably *is* sick,' the manager said. 'He could even die on a day like today if he's left there too long.'

'Here's the licence number,' Gloria said. She showed him her notebook.

' "Mighty-one"!' said the manager. 'Hmm!' He climbed into his booth and used the microphone.

'Will the owner of a car with the licence plate Mighty-one come to the manager's office?' he said.

Then he climbed down from the booth and stood with us, and we waited to see who would answer his call.

A man came towards us. He was the biggest man I ever saw. He must have been practically seven feet tall. He had two huge bags of groceries that he was balancing on his shoulders. He was wearing shorts, and a T-shirt that said RAMBO! He had muscles every place on his body that you could have a muscle, and he looked mean.

I pictured myself getting mashed, pictured Dad standing by my bed afterwards, shaking his head sadly and saying, 'Julian, you went too far.'

Huey looked from the man's toes up to his head and back down again, three times, and whispered to the store manager, 'When he gets here, why don't *you* talk?'

The manager smiled. 'You children just speak up,' he said. 'You can do it.'

'I'll do it,' Gloria said. 'I love dogs!'

Just then MIGHTY-1 came to a stop, practically on top of us and as big as a skyscraper.

He looked at the manager. 'So what did you call me for?' he asked.

Gloria looked up at him. 'You have a dog?' she asked.

'So what?' MIGHTY-1 said.

'It's too hot to leave him in a car with the windows rolled up. He could die,' Gloria said.

MIGHTY-1 glared at her. Then he glared at the manager. 'You called me over here to let three little *kids* mess in my business?'

'The children are right,' the manager said.

'Look,' said MIGHTY-1, pointing his finger down at the manager's nose. 'When I bought that dog, they told me

he was a strong, healthy dog. They didn't say anything about car windows. That dog is tough. He can take it.'

I hoped Gloria would say something more. But when I looked around, Gloria was gone!

MIGHTY-1 stuck his chin out. Then he stuck it back in so he could look down and see us.

'Didn't anybody ever tell you that kids should just mind their own business till they grow up? Especially your girlfriend!'

'She's not my girlfriend!' I said. 'She's my friend!'

I won't let anybody say I have a girlfriend – not even a huge, mean man who's seven feet tall.

'Friend or girlfriend,' MIGHTY-1 said. 'Makes no difference. You tell her—'

And then we all saw that Gloria was back.

'You!' MIGHTY-1 roared.

Gloria smiled her prettiest smile.

'Excuse me,' she said. 'I was checking your car. Your dog just fainted!'

MIGHTY-1's mouth hung open, like the door of a cave.

'Crumbles *fainted*!' he said. He dropped all his groceries and ran for the door.

Stuff rolled out of the grocery bags – a dozen rawhide fake dog bones, thirty-five cans of dog food, a ball with a bell inside, five boxes of Wheaties, Breakfast of Champions, a book called *How to Be a He-man*, and a magazine with an article called '79 Exercises for Your Toes'.

The manager started picking things up, and we helped him.

Suddenly the manager got a huge grin on his face, just the kind Huey gets. He picked up a book from the magazine rack and stuck it in one of the grocery bags, under the dog food cans.

The title was *How to Take Care of Your Dog*.

'Sometimes I have to do mischievous things,' he said. 'I just can't help myself. Now we need to take some water out to Crumbles,' he said.

So we went to the back of the store, put water in a bucket, and took it out to the car park.

Crumbles was lying on the ground in the shade. MIGHTY-1 was kneeling next to him, rubbing the dog's neck.

'We brought some water,' the manager said.

MIGHTY-1 looked up. 'Thank you,' he said.

The manager dunked Crumbles's head in the bucket of water. Then he held Crumbles's mouth open and poured some water into it.

Crumbles blinked.

'Crumbles! You're all right! You're going to be fine! Aren't you?' MIGHTY-1 said.

Crumbles made a little noise, something like a sigh.

'Oh, my sweet, adorable Crumbles!' said MIGHTY-1, and kissed him on the nose.

I Tell a Story

It was three days later, early in the morning. We hadn't got into any trouble for being secret agents so far. But nothing exciting had happened either.

Since we found Crumbles, we had checked the supermarket car parks often, looking for dead bodies and sick dogs. We hadn't found either. We had checked the bank about twenty times, hoping someone would rob it. Nobody had.

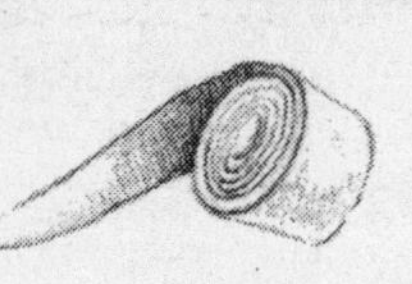

We were back at our secret meeting place in the park, trying to think of where we could find criminals.

'A known criminal might go to the hospital,' Gloria said. 'To get plastic surgery and change his or her face.'

'Let's go see who's getting surgery,' I said.

'They don't always let children in hospitals,' Gloria said.

I thought about that. I also thought about what Dad would say if he knew we were going to the hospital. I decided he wouldn't say anything. The hospital wasn't 'far'. It was right downtown.

'It's a good idea to go,' I said. 'If anyone asks us, we could say we're there because your mother is going to have a baby.'

'Why should it be *my* mother?' Gloria demanded. 'Why not *your* mother?'

'If our mother ever found out about it, she might not like that story,' Huey said.

'My mother wouldn't like it either,' Gloria said.

'We aren't supposed to make up stories,' Huey said. 'Especially you, Julian.'

'Suppose we just go, and we don't make up any story?' I said. 'Suppose we just look around fast?'

'OK,' Gloria said.

'OK,' Huey said.

Ten minutes later we went through the door of the hospital. We passed the lobby and the gift shop, where people buy presents for their sick relatives and friends. We passed a nursing station. A nurse looked at us. Question marks were spinning in her eyes.

'We're going to see her mother,' I explained, pointing to Gloria.

I kept walking fast.

'Julian,' Gloria said. 'Did you *have* to say that?'

'Somebody had to make a sacrifice,' I whispered. 'It just happened to be you.'

We saw a sign painted in black

letters on the wall. It said SURGERY. There was a big black arrow next to it, pointing straight ahead.

We started to slow down.

There were patients in the hall, walking slowly, wearing pyjamas.

It didn't look as if their faces had been changed recently.

'Excuse me,' Gloria said to one man. 'What are you having?'

'I had it,' said the man. 'Appendix. Out.' He made a gesture with his hand, as if he was pulling something out of his right side.

'Ugh,' Huey said.

'Believe me,' said the man, 'it was better out than in. What are you kids doing here?'

'We're visiting *their* mother,' Gloria said.

'Maybe you should ask the nurse if you're in the right section,' said the man. 'Oh, Nurse!' he called.

'Make like a tree!' I said.

'A *tree*?' Huey said. 'I'm not a *tree*!'

'Huey!' I said. *'Leave!'* And I pulled him by the hand.

'I hope you're better soon!' Gloria called to the man with his appendix out.

We zoomed to a sign marked EXIT as fast as we could go.

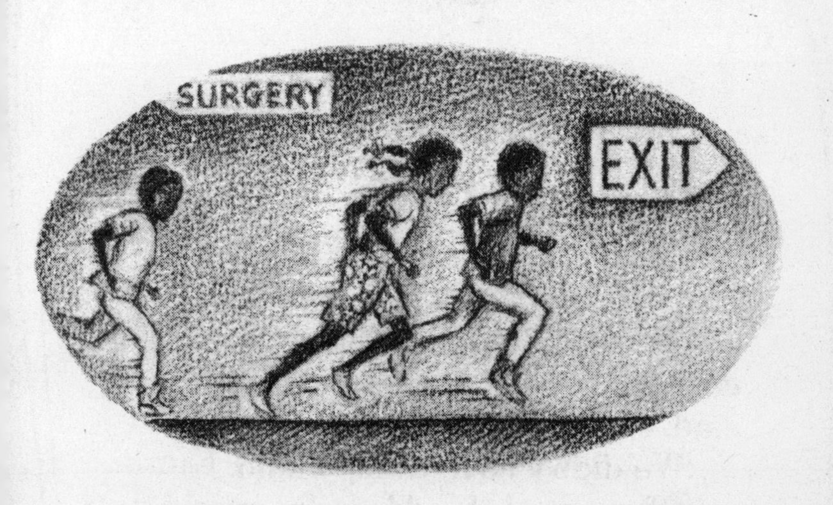

We Capture the Great Goo-Goo

Outside, on the grounds around the hospital, we caught our breath.

'We didn't really check very many criminals – I mean, patients,' Huey said.

'We didn't have time,' I said.

'Of course,' I added, 'a criminal

could have seen us coming. In fact, a criminal could be out here, hiding in the bushes, right now.'

Just as I said that, a big hedge in front of us started to shake back and forth.

'There's somebody!' Gloria said.

Together, very slowly, very quietly, we started moving up on the hedge.

When we got there, we didn't see anybody. But the hedge was shaking again, farther down – as if it were waving to us.

'Faster this time!' I said, and we ran.

When we got to the other strange spot in the hedge, no-one was there, either. But right next to it was a very young kid in shorts – the kind of kid who has just learned to walk and goes really fast so he won't fall over.

We watched him. He was heading for the hospital fountain. He got to it and just kept walking. Pretty soon he was in water up to his knees.

He turned around and smiled at us.

'Goo-goo,' he said.

'Goo-Goo,' Gloria said, 'are you coming out of there?'

Goo-Goo just stared.

'Are you coming out of there?' Gloria repeated.

'No!' Goo-Goo said.

'Do you know how to swim?' Gloria said.

'No!' Goo-Goo said.

'Does your mother know where you are?' Huey asked.

'No!' Goo-Goo said.

'Maybe he'll be all right in there,' I said.

'Are you crazy?' Gloria said.

'No!' Goo-Goo said.

'Will you come with us?' Gloria asked.

'*No!*' Goo-Goo said.

'What are we going to do?' Gloria said. 'If we leave him, he might drown. If we take him out, he'll start to cry. People might think we're kidnapping him.'

'We have to try psychology,' I said.

'You'd *like* to come out of the water, wouldn't you, Goo-Goo?' I said. I smiled a big smile.

Goo-Goo smiled back. 'No!' he said. He splashed at us a little.

'Psychology is not working,' Gloria whispered.

'You're right!' I said. 'It's not.' I was worried. I started pulling at the chain around my neck, the chain with my lucky coin on it.

All at once I had an idea. I climbed up on the edge of the fountain. I took the chain off. I made my lucky coin swing back and forth in front of Goo-Goo's eyes.

First Goo-Goo's eyes, and then his head, started rolling back and forth. His hand reached out towards the chain.

'You stay right there, Goo-Goo!' I told him.

'No!' Goo-Goo said.

I moved my chain to the edge of the

fountain. Goo-Goo reached for it. I stepped back on to the grass. Goo-Goo got out of the fountain.

I made my coin sway one more time in front of his eyes. Goo-Goo's head swayed, and he moved towards me.

I kept backing up, with Gloria and Huey right next to me. Goo-Goo followed us all the way through the hospital entrance.

We heard a voice from the gift shop. '. . . I don't know which way he ran! And I will lose my mind if I don't find him!'

Goo-Goo looked up and forgot about my lucky coin. He staggered into the gift shop on his short, fat legs, dripping water on to the floor.

'My baby!' said a woman. 'You found him!'

'We brought him in,' I said. 'Sorry we had to hypnotize him to do it.'

'He was playing in the fountain,' Gloria said. 'We didn't think he could swim.'

'He *can't* swim,' said the woman. 'I'm so grateful! I'm so glad he's safe!' She squeezed some water out of his hair.

'His name is Walter Albert Sims the Third, and the only word that he can say is—'

'No!' said the Great Goo-Goo.

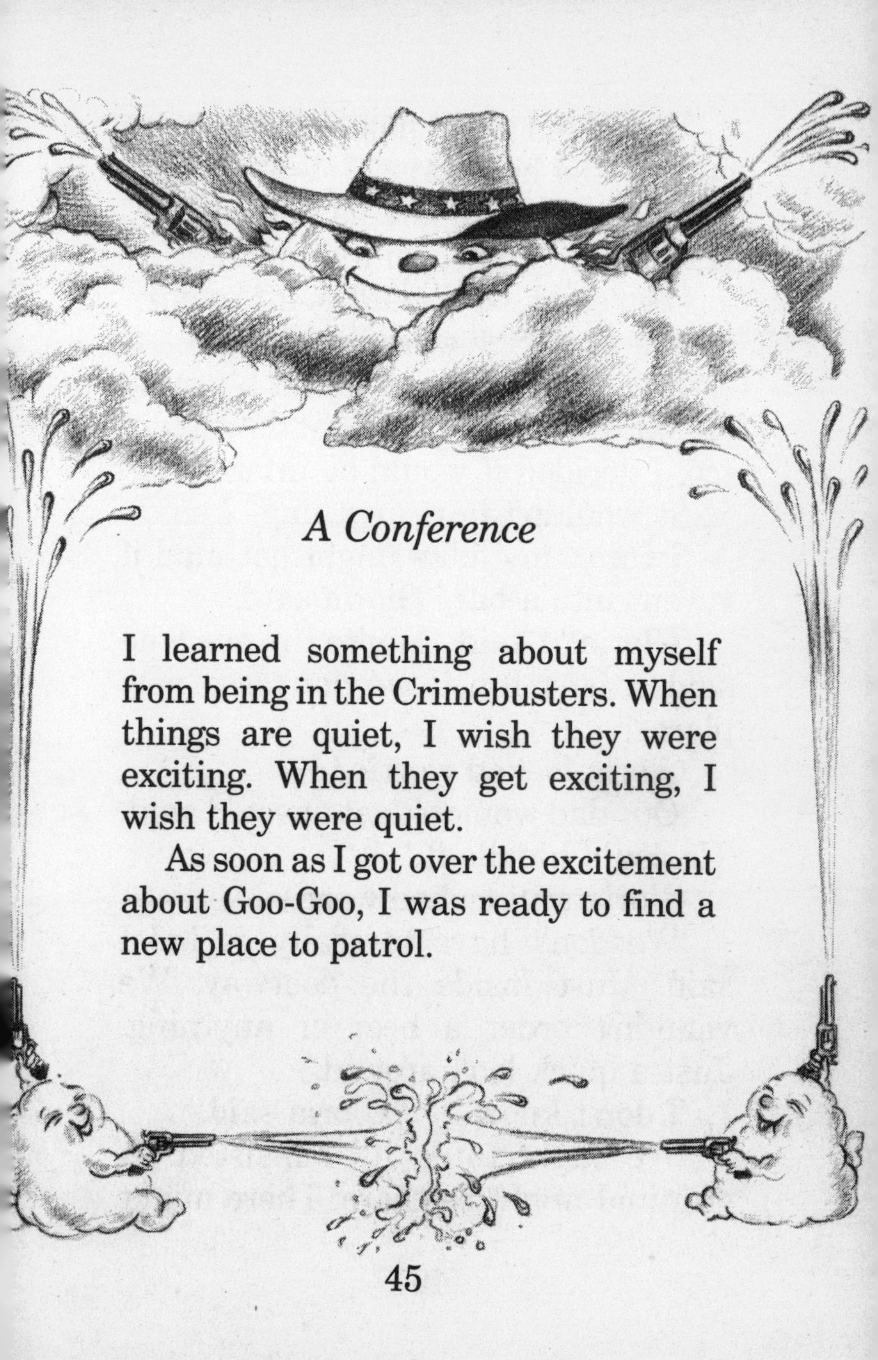

A Conference

I learned something about myself from being in the Crimebusters. When things are quiet, I wish they were exciting. When they get exciting, I wish they were quiet.

As soon as I got over the excitement about Goo-Goo, I was ready to find a new place to patrol.

We talked about it on the pavement outside the hospital.

'A criminal might go into a bar,' Huey said. 'To drown his sorrows.'

'You think we should go into a *bar*?' Gloria said. She sounded scared.

I wondered if that would be going too far. But bars were right downtown too. I decided it would be interesting.

'It wouldn't hurt anything,' I said.

'I think my folks might get mad if I went into a bar,' Gloria said.

'Gloria!' I said. 'You're the one who said it isn't fun if we don't see new places!'

Gloria looked worried.

'Our dad wouldn't get upset,' I said. 'He could handle it.'

Gloria still looked worried.

'We don't have to really go in,' I said. 'Just inside the doorway. We wouldn't order a beer or anything. Just a quick look around.'

'I don't know . . .' Gloria said.

'We ought to do it,' I insisted. 'A criminal might be there. There might be a shootout, like in cowboy movies. Just think of that!

'Let's go!' I said.

There was perspiration on Gloria's forehead. I didn't think it was just from the heat.

'All for one, one for all,' she said.

I led the way.

Trees Again

Seven minutes later we were at the doorway of a bar. It had a sign with a ram's head painted on it. The letters at the bottom of the sign said SHEEPSHEAD LOUNGE.

'Ready?' I asked.

'Ready as I'll ever be,' Gloria said.

I opened the door a crack. Nice cool air and a beery smell came out. I stepped inside. Huey followed me. Gloria tried to hide behind Huey.

We looked around. It was dark and

dim inside. There was a barman in a white shirt, and a hundred shiny bottles behind the bar. At one table two men were having ham and eggs and toast and coffee. At another there were four old men playing cards. They each had a glass of beer, but it didn't look as if they were going to shoot each other anytime soon.

'OK,' Gloria whispered. 'We did it. Let's go!'

'Just a minute,' I whispered back. 'I want to get a closer look at all the faces.'

But just as I was doing that, they all started to stare at us.

'Looking for anybody in particular?' the barman said.

'Not exactly,' I said.

'Then look at that sign up there,' he said.

I looked. The sign said UNDER 18 NOT ADMITTED BY LAW.

'That sign means *you*,' the barman said.

'Lawbreaking!' Gloria moaned.

One of the men with ham and eggs put down his fork.

'Hey,' he called, 'aren't you Ralph Bates's boys?'

I wanted to keep Huey from answering. 'Huey,' I said. 'AA!' But I figured that wasn't enough. 'Make like a tree!' I whispered.

Huey made like a tree.

All his limbs shook. He grew roots. 'No!' he called to the ham-and-eggs man. 'No! No way! We don't even know Dad!'

'Huey! Run!' I said.

He ran fast, and so did I. But Gloria was a whole block ahead of us.

We Watch the Wizard

We ran until we couldn't run any more. If there hadn't been a building to fall against, we'd have dropped on the pavement. Instead, we propped ourselves against a wall and breathed hard.

'It'll probably be all right,' I said. 'We didn't actually go *in* the bar – I mean, way in. We didn't order a beer or anything. If the ham-and-eggs man mentions us to Dad, and Dad talks to us, we can just say . . .' I didn't know what.

'We can just say we wanted to see what a bar looks like,' Huey suggested.

'That might work,' I said. I didn't want to worry any more. It was too hot to worry.

Gloria wiped her face with her hand. 'I sure am thirsty,' she said. 'I sure could use a drink! I mean, a *soft* drink.'

I looked around. Across the street was a big sign. It said:

KINGMAN'S CAFÉ,
AIR-CONDITIONED

'We could go in there,' I said.

'OK,' Gloria said.

We staggered on over.

Gloria breathed deeply. 'It's nice and cool in here,' she said.

We were sitting in a big wooden booth back in the corner. The air conditioner was above us, clanking every now and then. Besides the air conditioner, there were ceiling fans, a jukebox, a painting of a green forest on the back wall, and a long counter with the kind of stools that spin around. Behind the counter was a big opening to the kitchen. There was a conveyor belt that led from the kitchen to the front counter, but there wasn't a single person in sight.

'Is there a waiter?' I said.

'No,' answered a voice.

'Could you bring us a menu?' Gloria asked.

'Nope,' answered the voice.

'Is this a *restaurant*?' Huey asked.

'The best!' said the voice. 'It's the best, because I'm the best,' the voice continued. 'I'm the Food Wizard. I know what people want before *they* know. For instance, I know you. Water types, right?'

And three glasses of water with ice and straws skidded down the conveyor belt on a tray, got to the bottom, and bumped on to the long counter.

'You want 'em,' said the Wizard, 'go get 'em.'

We got up and went to the counter and finished off the water. Three more glasses came down the ramp on another tray. We decided to drink those at the counter, so maybe we could see the Wizard. But he was still out of sight.

'This place is *modern*,' said the voice of the Food Wizard. 'For instance, I am speaking to you now from the walk-in refrigerator, which is the perfect place for a summer

vacation in this town. For instance, I don't even have to leave the walk-in refrigerator to answer the telephone. It's a speaker phone. It goes on by itself. Like now.'

We heard a little ring, and then a different voice – a voice on the phone line.

'TJ, this is Barry. One club sandwich with cheddar.'

'Teddy Bear,' said another voice, 'this is Nemo. Egg salad, pizza sandwich, root beer, chips.'

'Knuckleball,' said a third voice, 'this is Harry. Roast beef on rye, pickles, Chinese rice, tea.'

'Ted,' said a fourth voice, 'this is Art. Swiss cheese with turkey, coleslaw, and radishes.'

'Eddie,' said a fifth voice, 'this is Rick. One corned beef on wholewheat.'

'Junior, this is Harvey. Liver and onions, Waldorf salad on the side.'

The phone clicked off.

'Friends,' said the voice of the

Wizard. 'They're building a house. They call in their orders. Then they come to pick them up.'

It was hard to talk to the Wizard, since his voice was coming out of a loudspeaker, but Gloria tried.

'So you write down the orders now?' she asked.

'Never!' said the Food Wizard. 'I just remember 'em. It's good mental training. Along about two, when the rush is over, I write 'em down. You want to know where the menu is, check the timepiece.'

'The what?' Huey said.

'Clock, to you,' said the Wizard. 'On the wall.'

We found the clock and started reading the menu next to it.

No matter what I ordered, my pocket money would be wiped out.

'Don't know what you want, do you?' asked the Wizard. 'I figured you for no-spend types.'

His voice wasn't coming out of the loudspeaker any more. It was coming out of the kitchen. We turned around to see him, but all we saw was his back – white pants, white shirt, and a tall white chef's hat. He was moving fast, and his arms were a blur. He had a butter knife in one hand, a pepper grinder in the other, and three slices of bread in the air. There were clouds of smoke and steam, and the smells of hamburger, roast beef, pizza, and liver and onions were all scrambling and swirling around.

'You're fast!' Huey told the Wizard.

'Huh!' said the Wizard. 'You haven't seen anything yet! Watch this!

'You take a tear potato,' said the Wizard, 'and—'

'Tear potato?' I said.

'Yeah, the kind that makes you cry.

And you slice it into rushin' rings.'

We got up on the revolving stools to see; it looked like the Wizard was slicing something, but we couldn't tell what.

'Russian rings?' said Gloria.

'Yeah,' said the Wizard. 'Make 'em in a rush. And then you gold-plate your rings' – his hands swept something through something else that was in a bowl – 'and you drop your rings in that think tank.'

'Think tank?' said Huey.

'That's where the tear potato gets its last chance to think about its life,' explained the Wizard.

'Then you rack your rings' – a basket came out of the think tank – 'drain, and serve. Three minutes,

minus ten seconds,' said the Wizard. 'Rushin' rings. Try 'em. No charge.'

One large plate came rolling down the conveyor belt on to the counter.

'French-fried onion rings!' Gloria said.

'Some folks call 'em that,' said the Wizard. 'Myself, I call 'em rushin' rings. Now, with these I always like sad apples.'

'Sad apples!' I repeated.

'That's right,' said the Wizard. 'Terminally squeezed.'

He walked to the door of the walk-in refrigerator. In a second, three glasses of apple juice rolled down the conveyor belt.

'Free sample. No charge,' said the Wizard. 'Eat up. But you gotta go

before twelve, when the lunch crowd comes in. There's no room after that.'

He turned around and smiled at us. He was a young man, maybe nineteen or twenty years old. He had a friendly face. There was a little scar above his upper lip. I thought I'd seen his face someplace before, but I couldn't remember where.

I took five rushin' rings at once.

'These are great!' I said.

'*Bon appétit!*' said the Wizard. He turned back to the kitchen, picking up a spatula in one hand and a spoon in the other. With his foot he pressed a button that turned on the jukebox.

'My favourite song,' explained the Wizard. 'Free sample.'

'It's a long road,' sang the singer on

the jukebox. 'A long, long road I'm travelling, but there's light at the end of the trail.'

We finished the rushin' rings. I left five cents tip.

'Thanks a lot,' we said. 'We were thirsty.'

'Drop by again when you're Thursday,' said the Wizard. 'Just not when I'm Russian.'

Out on the street the heat wrapped around us.

'He's nice!' Huey said.

'He has a nice face,' Gloria said. 'Even his little scar looks nice.'

Then I remembered where I had seen a face like the Wizard's – on one of the wanted posters at the post office – the one for Eugene George Johnson, 'the Great Imitator'!

We Report

'But how can we be sure?' Gloria asked. We were standing on the street corner, trying to decide what to do.

'We should go back to the post office and check Eugene George Johnson's wanted sheet,' I said.

We ran to the post office as fast as

we could. The sheet on Eugene George Johnson was still there. We studied the facts. They all matched. Eugene spoke a strange private language. So did the Wizard. Eugene used many different names. So did the Wizard. Eugene's hobby was cooking. So was the Wizard's. Eugene travelled a lot; the Wizard liked a song about travelling. Eugene had a little scar above his upper lip. So did the Wizard.

We studied the photos of Eugene.

'He could be the Wizard,' Gloria said. 'Then again, he might not be.'

'I think the Wizard *is* Eugene,' I said. 'Everything fits, even the scar.'

'But are you sure the Wizard's scar is one quarter of an inch above his upper lip?' Gloria asked.

'Gloria,' I answered, 'what can we do? We can't go to the Wizard and say, "May we measure your scar with this ruler?" We need to give the police our information.'

'Us . . . actually . . . go . . . see . . . the . . . *police*?' Gloria said.

Huey said, 'We never heard anybody call the Wizard Eugene.'

'Huey!' I said. 'That's the one name he *wouldn't* use.'

'We didn't hear him speak Chinese,' Gloria said.

'He cooks Chinese rice!' I said. 'Isn't that enough?'

'He was nice to us,' Huey said sadly.

'But he could still be a criminal,' I said. 'Besides, look at this.' I pointed to the very bottom of the sheet, where it said in big letters: $25,000 REWARD.

We walked to the police station, saying, 'All for one, one for all.' I had caught hold of Gloria's and Huey's hands. They weren't walking fast.

We got to the police-station door.

'Gloria,' I said, 'I'm sure we're right!'

'We're going to be heroes,' Gloria said. 'Or else the opposite.'

I went ahead. I opened the door.

Inside, the police station was not scary. There were five desks, three with empty paper cups on them and all with pictures of police officers and their families. Against the wall were

big drawers of files, probably with centuries of crimes described inside. There was a sign that said DO EVERYONE A FAVOUR: DON'T SMOKE and another that said YOUR MOTHER DOES NOT WORK HERE. PLEASE CLEAN UP AFTER YOURSELF!

The only scary part was the receptionist who was talking to us. 'What may I do for you?' she asked.

'We'd like to speak to a police officer,' I said.

'All the officers are out on call,' the receptionist said. 'But you can speak to the chief.'

'The chief!' Gloria moaned.

'All right,' I said.

The receptionist picked up her intercom phone.

'Three children here to see you,' she said.

She listened to the chief say something. Then she smiled at us. 'Go straight down the hall. It's the first room on the left.'

We walked down the hall. My feet were feeling kind of weak and slithery, and I had spaghetti-string legs. I was still holding Gloria's and Huey's hands.

We went into the first room on the left.

The chief was sitting behind a big desk. He had a nice face but some grey hair. I could understand that. I figured that if I kept on being a secret agent, I would soon have grey hair too. On the desk was a nameplate – THEODORE J. DAVIS, SR, CHIEF OF POLICE.

We stood in front of the desk. Huey didn't say a word. Gloria looked green.

'I'm Julian,' I said. 'Julian Bates.' Gloria and Huey didn't say their names.

I knew I was right, but it was still hard to keep talking.

'We're here about a most-wanted case,' I said.

'Sit down,' said the chief. 'Get comfortable.'

THEODORE J. DAVIS, SR.
CHIEF OF POLICE

We all sat down, but I didn't feel too comfortable.

'Now,' said the chief, 'tell me: which wanted person have you found?'

'We think we have found Eugene George Johnson,' I said.

The chief smiled. 'Eugene? "The Great Imitator"?' he said. 'You've really found him? He's someone I definitely would like to capture. And there's a twenty-five-thousand-dollar reward! Of course, if *you* have found him, the reward is yours. Where is he?'

'He's in Kingman's Café,' I said.

'In Kingman's Café!' repeated the chief. 'But that's the café where the service is faster than the speed of time. You mean, he *was* in Kingman's!'

The chief started to get out of his chair.

'There's not so much hurry,' I said. 'See, he *works* in Kingman's.'

'Kingman was talking about

adding extra help,' said the chief. 'Is it somebody new?'

'We don't know,' Gloria said. 'When we were there, only one man was working. A young man or an old boy.'

'Wait a minute!' said the chief. He looked shocked. 'You're not talking about T. J. Teddy Bear Knuckleball Ted Eddie Junior?'

'Right!' Huey said. 'He's the one!'

'Hard to believe!' said the chief. He looked at us sternly, as if he could see everything about us, from our fingerprints to our toeprints.

'You three go by the post office much?' he said.

'Sometimes,' I said.

'You've been studying Eugene's poster?' he said.

'Sometimes,' I said.

'You're a private investigating group?' he said.

I didn't want to answer. I was afraid the chief would say kids should just mind their own business.

'Are you! Or aren't you?' said the chief.

'We are, kind of,' I said.

'Good!' said the chief.

I was relieved he wasn't mad at us.

'Good!' said the chief. 'Because I have to investigate T. J. Teddy Bear Knuckleball Ted Eddie Junior. And I want *you* to do it for me.'

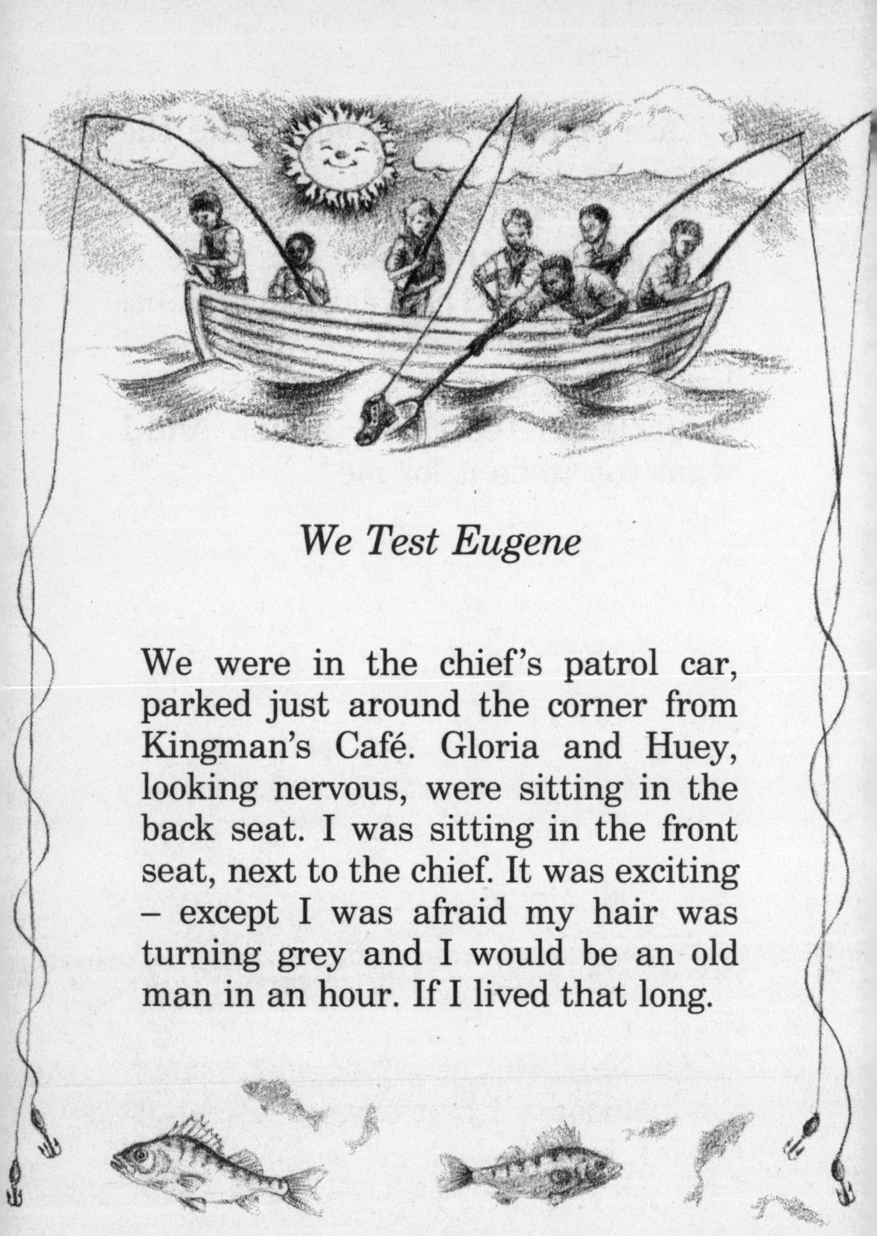

We Test Eugene

We were in the chief's patrol car, parked just around the corner from Kingman's Café. Gloria and Huey, looking nervous, were sitting in the back seat. I was sitting in the front seat, next to the chief. It was exciting – except I was afraid my hair was turning grey and I would be an old man in an hour. If I lived that long.

'Now, here's what I want you to do,' said the chief. 'Go in and sit at the counter. Order some lunch. You don't have to pay for it. When I come in – later – I'll pay for it.

'After you order the lunch, you start questioning the suspect. Just ask him about his life in a friendly way. Ask him what he was doing on April twenty-first. That's the date of Eugene's last strike. In Topeka, Kansas.

'Then ask him if he knows Eugene George Johnson. Watch his face when he answers.'

'Maybe – maybe you'd lend us your gun,' I said.

'Sorry, I can't do that,' said the chief. 'I'll give you this whistle. If you have a problem – if the suspect gets a little wild or crazy – blow hard. I'll be right in.'

The chief reached over and opened the car door – because I didn't open it myself, I guess.

Huey tapped the chief on the

shoulder. 'May I stay here with you?' he said.

The chief smiled. 'Sorry, son,' he said. 'I need all three of you working the café. Have a nice lunch.'

'I was hungry,' Gloria said. 'I'm not hungry any more.'

We sat down on stools at the counter. I held the chief's police whistle hidden tight in my palm.

'You three!' said the Wizard. 'Back again!'

'Yes,' I said. 'And we want three barbecued beefs on buns.'

'Come into some money, have you?' said the Wizard.

'Kind of,' I said.

'By the way,' I said. 'What's your life like? I mean, what do you do with your life?'

'What do I do with my life?' said the Wizard. 'Same as everybody else.'

An answer like that wouldn't satisfy the chief.

'What do you mean?' I said.

'Same as everybody else. I work.'

'Don't you do anything else besides work?' I asked.

'I get up at six-thirty. I go to the gym, I swim, I lift weights. I come here. I work eight hours. After that I go to college, and after that I go out with my girlfriend. Then I go home, I go to bed, I get up at six-thirty, I go to the gym . . . Get the picture?' said the Wizard.

'Don't you do anything else? Anything – more?' I asked.

'No!' said the Wizard. He turned around and started stirring the barbecue.

'I like to travel so much,' Gloria said. 'Especially to Topeka, Kansas. How about you? Have you ever been to Topeka?'

'It's a nice town,' said the Wizard. He turned around and faced us.

Huey opened his mouth. 'Have you ever heard of – of – of – of—'

'Eugene George Johnson?' I finished.

'Sure have,' said the Wizard. 'A tricky mover! I admire him!'

'You *do*?' I said. My hand tightened hard around the whistle.

'You mean the basketball player, don't you?' the Wizard said.

'That's not who I meant,' I said.

The Wizard turned his back to us and peered into the barbecue pot again.

'Burner's acting up. Not heating

fast today,' he said. 'It was working fine till April.'

'That reminds me,' I said. 'My favourite day is April twenty-first. Do you remember what *you* were doing on April twenty-first?'

'Sure do!' said the Wizard. 'I wasn't here. I was living for free, having a great vacation.'

'In Topeka?' Gloria said.

'Girl,' said the Wizard, 'you got Topeka on the brain?'

'You *weren't* in Topeka?' Gloria said.

'I was up the river, on a fishing trip with a Boy Scout troop.'

'Really?' I said. The Wizard was OK. He had an alibi. I was a tiny bit sorry, but mostly glad.

'Finally hot,' said the Wizard. He ladled out the barbecue. 'You kids sure are hard on the Wizard,' he said. 'You come here in the morning, you act normal. Poor, but normal. Now all of a sudden you come back with money and more questions than newspaper reporters! You aren't on drugs, I hope?'

'Us!' Gloria said.

'For your own good, I'd have to turn you in. Because I have certain connections,' said the Wizard. 'In fact—'

The door to the café opened. We smiled. We were rescued. It was the chief.

The Wizard smiled too. 'Hi, Dad!' he said.

The whistle dropped from my hand.

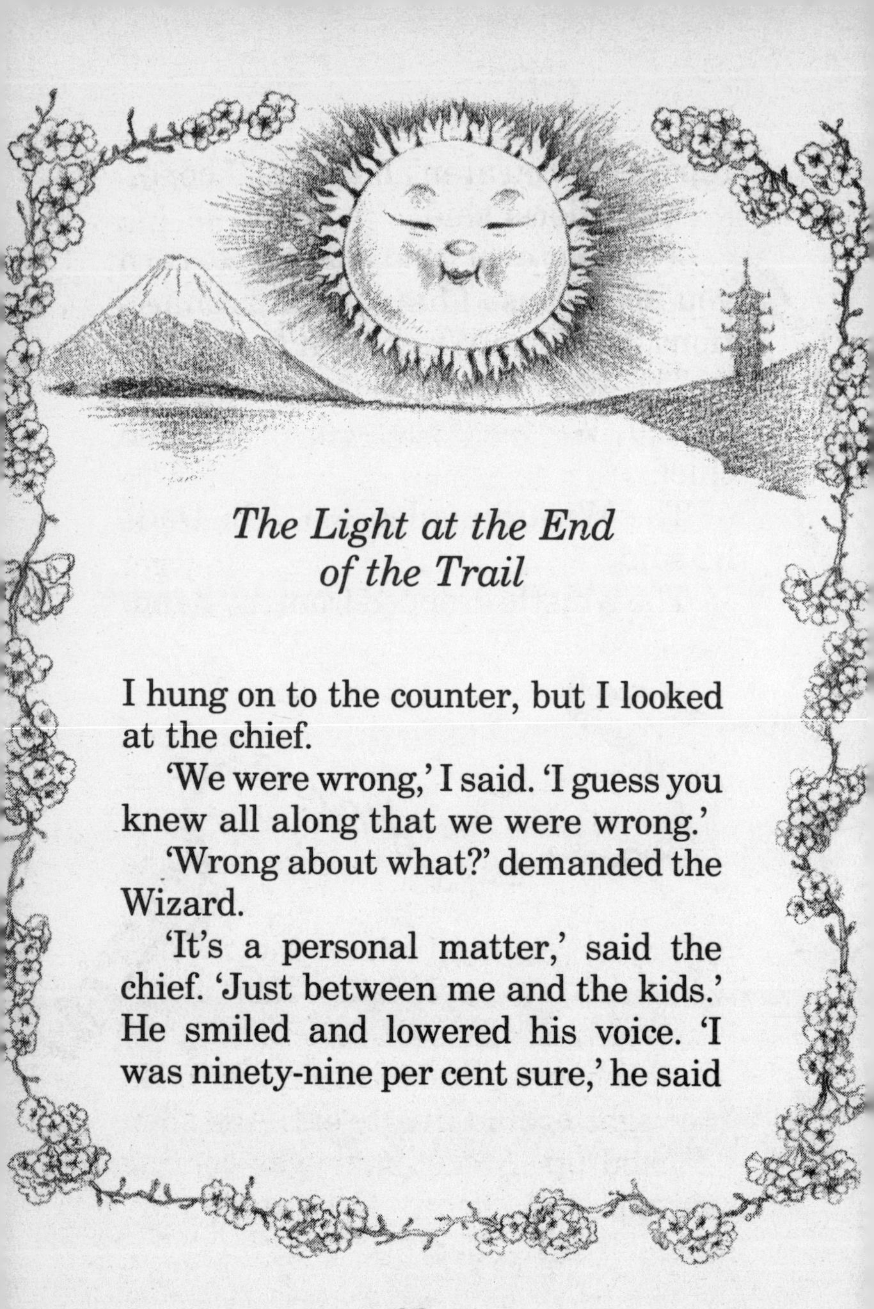

The Light at the End of the Trail

I hung on to the counter, but I looked at the chief.

'We were wrong,' I said. 'I guess you knew all along that we were wrong.'

'Wrong about what?' demanded the Wizard.

'It's a personal matter,' said the chief. 'Just between me and the kids.' He smiled and lowered his voice. 'I was ninety-nine per cent sure,' he said to us. 'But it's my job to be one hundred per cent sure.' He lowered his voice even more. 'No matter who the suspect is.'

'Dad,' the Wizard said. 'You *know* these kids? These kids are *strange*.'

'They act a little strange,' said the chief. 'But it's only because they're working for me. I'm teaching them not to decide about anything until they get the facts. TJ, do you have more of that barbecue?'

'Coming up,' the Wizard said.

'We're going to move the kids' food over to a booth,' the chief said. 'I want to sit with them.'

So we moved all our plates, and the chief ordered some sad apples, and rushin' rings, and Chinese rice. While we waited we told the chief about Crumbles and Baby Goo-Goo.

My appetite started to come back. I thought I could finally eat. And then I looked up. A customer was coming through the door. I blinked. My stomach shrivelled up.

KINGMAN'S

'Hi, Dad,' Huey and I said.

Dad didn't even say 'hi' back.

'I go by the hospital,' he said. 'I go by to talk about a car part with a customer who had his appendix out. He asks if I have a son named Huey. I say yes, and he says a boy named Huey was just in there with another boy, and they both look a lot like me. And they were with a girl. Then he says, "Too bad your wife is in the hospital!" And I say, "She isn't!"

'Then I stop by the Sheepshead Lounge to look for a customer who owes me money, and a man says, "Your sons were just in here."

'Then I think, Well, my sons sure are getting around. And I come into Kingman's to think it over, and here you are, having lunch with the chief of police! So naturally I wonder *what* is going on.'

Dad looked at me. I cleared my throat. It seemed like there was going to be an awful lot to explain.

'Why don't you sit right down with

us, Mr Bates?' said the chief. 'Order yourself some lunch.'

Dad pulled a chair up to the booth and sat on it with both his legs out to the side, as if he were riding a horse. He didn't look calm.

'Don't worry, Mr Bates,' the chief said. 'Your boys and Gloria have been helping me on a case, so I bought them lunch. They are very fine children, all three of them. Very smart, and very alert. In fact, they saved a dying dog, and over at the hospital they saved a boy from drowning.'

'Really!' Dad said.

'Tell your dad about it,' said the chief.

So I did. Dad wanted all the details, and he was really impressed, and while we talked we had more sad apples, and more barbecue, and more of everything, and it was really a great day.

When we couldn't talk or eat any more, we said goodbye to the Wizard. The chief shook hands with us and said he hoped we could work together again sometime. On the way out Dad put his arm around us and told us he was proud of us.

So I decided it was safe to ask him a few things.

'You aren't angry that we went into a bar?' I said.

'A bar isn't a place for kids,' he said. 'But I can understand that you wanted to see it. It's no big deal. I don't think Gloria's folks will be mad at her, either.' He gave Gloria a little hug.

'Another thing,' I said. 'You aren't mad that we went too far?'

'Too far?' said my dad. 'What do you mean "too far"?'

'You told me, when I got my bike, not to go too far. And we went almost all over town.'

'Oh, that!' said my father. 'I guess I never finished explaining. I meant: not along the bypass, and not across the railway tracks, and not under the big bridge where there are lots of trucks. That's what I meant.'

Huey looked up. 'So we *can* go to Tokyo!' he said.

'Tokyo?' Dad said.

I realized it was no time to say 'AA'. I stepped on Huey's foot.

THE END

JULIAN, DREAM DOCTOR

Ann Cameron

'This is what I've always dreamed of! Julian, you're a genius! This is the most unforgettable birthday present that I have ever had!'

Julian wants more than anything to make his dad's birthday the best ever. That means getting him a very special gift - and finding out just what his dad has always dreamed of isn't going to be easy. With the help of Huey and Gloria, Julian sets out to arrange a birthday party with a rather unusual present - if they can catch it first!

A lively and entertaining tale about Julian, a boy with a talent for getting into mischief!

ISBN 0552 548251

THE JULIAN STORIES

by Ann Cameron

'It's such a big pudding,' Huey said. 'It can't hurt to have a little more . . .'

Julian just can't resist a little taste of the wonderful lemon pudding his father has made. But as he and his little brother, Huey, taste just a little bit more, the pudding is suddenly all gone! And Julian is in trouble . . .

Six funny and lively tales in which Julian gets into mischief – and out again – and finally makes a special new friend.

'Beautiful, bold, black and white illustrations match the tone and humour of the stories' *The Times Literary Supplement*

0 440 863333

HUEY'S TIGER

Ann Cameron

"Do you want to go to Africa, Tiger?"

Huey wants to be a wild-animal tracker, like his big brother Julian. But Julian tells Huey he is too little, and talks too much. So Huey decides to prove just how clever and brave he is, and he sets off for Africa, where the wild animals are. On the way, he makes friends with the little dog, Tiger. But which way is Africa?

Fans of the popular Julian Stories series will recognize Huey as Julian's irrepressible younger brother. Now Huey tells his own stories in this warm and humorous collection. There are more of Huey's stories in *Banana Spaghetti*.

ISBN 0 552 54577 5

BANANA SPAGHETTI

Ann Cameron

"It's a new invention... banana spaghetti!"

Huey wants to surprise his mum on Mother's Day, so he invents banana spaghetti! It takes a bit of help from Dad to get it right, but Huey is determined to show everyone that he is just as clever as his big brother, Julian. And when Huey beats his fear of the dark, and copes with a dead fish, he proves he is just as brave too.

Fans of the popular Julian Stories series will recognize Huey as Julian's irrepressible younger brother. Now Huey tells his own stories in this warm and humorous collection.

'Filled with ingenious details and written in a beguiling style' *Junior Bookshelf*

ISBN 0 552 545767

THE FIREWORK-MAKER'S DAUGHTER

by Philip Pullman

'You want to be a Firework-Maker? Walk into my flames!'

More than anything else in the world, Lila wants to be a Firework-Maker. But every Firework-Maker must make a perilous journey to face the terrifying Fire-Fiend! Can Lila possibly survive? Especially when she doesn't know she needs special protection to survive his flames . . .

A gripping and action-packed adventure, filled with fun and entertaining characters.

'One of those rare books with a confident magic all their own . . . superbly illustrated . . . sheer genius' *Independent*

WINNER OF THE GOLD MEDAL FOR THE 1996 SMARTIES BOOK PRIZE, 9-11 AGE CATEGORY

0 440 863317

ROOM 13

by Robert Swindells

The night before her school trip, Fliss has a terrible nightmare about a dark, sinister house – a house with a ghastly secret in room thirteen. Arriving in Whitby, she discovers that the hotel they will be staying in looks very like the house in the dream. There is one important difference – there is no room thirteen.

Or is there? At the stroke of midnight, something strange happens to the linen cupboard on the dim landing. Something strange is happening to Ellie-May Sunderland too, and Fliss and her friends find themselves drawn into a desperate bid to save her.

A spooky adventure, full of fun and thrills, from the author of the award-winning *Brother in the Land.*

0 440 862272

OPERATION GADGETMAN!

by Malorie Blackman

BOOM! WHIZZ! KER-BOOM!

Beans calls her dad 'Gadgetman' because of the weird and wonderful gadgets he comes up with – everything from exploding biscuits to Spy Kits. But when Gadgetman accidentally invents a device that could be used to steal millions of pounds, he is suddenly in terrible danger. For the wrong people find out and Gadgetman goes missing – kidnapped!

Can Beans track down the kidnappers and find Gadgetman before he is forced to hand over the details of his invention? With the help of her friends, Ann and Louisa, and her special Gadgetman Spy Kit, she is determined to try . . .

'An exciting thriller, with code-breaking schoolgirl detectives' *Guardian*

0 440 863074